Case of the MISSING CAT

Written by Janet Palazzo-Craig
Illustrated by Ellen Shire

Troll Associates

Library of Congress Cataloging in Publication Data

Palazzo-Craig, Janet.
   Case of the missing cat.

   (A Troll easy-to-read mystery)
   Summary: Richard's cat, Crumpet, is missing and
his friends help him look for her.
   [1. Mystery and detective stories. 2. Cats—
Fiction] I. Shire, Ellen, ill. II. Title.
III. Series: Troll easy-to-read mystery.
PZ7.P1762Cas   [Fic]   81-7635
ISBN 0-89375-594-X (case)   AACR2
ISBN 0-89375-595-8 (pbk.)

Case of the
MISSING CAT

It's funny how things happen. Like, for instance, how I became a famous detective. I didn't ask to be one. It just happened.

I was out running one morning. I thought I would run to the park. Then I would have pancakes for breakfast — lots of them-with blueberry syrup and butter.

I was running along. My sneakers felt good. My sweatshirt felt good. I felt good. Those pancakes would make me feel even better.

I heard a bike behind me. It had
training wheels. It could only be one
person. Richard. I ran a little faster.
Richard rode his bike a little faster.

"Guess what?" Richard asked. He didn't wait for me to guess. He never does. "Someone took my cat. Someone took Crumpet."

To tell you the truth, I wasn't too broken up over the news. Crumpet is a black and white cat. Crumpet is not very friendly. Crumpet hisses — and scratches. Crumpet is not my favorite cat.

"Can you help me find her?" asked Richard. I ran a little faster. Richard rode a little faster. I knew when I was beaten.

"What makes you think someone took her?" I asked.

"She didn't come home for dinner last night. She always comes home for dinner, especially when we are having tuna fish," Richard said.

Like I said, I know when I'm beaten. "Okay, Richard," I said, "after breakfast, I'll come over to your house. Then I shall find the missing Crumpet."

After breakfast, I started toward Richard's house. But on my way, I saw something strange. I saw a brown cat, a red cat, a white cat, and a black cat. All together. Sitting in a row. Waiting outside a door. Something was fishy! And I'm not kidding. There was this smell—like fish.

Like they say, "the nose knows." My
nose told me this was the clue I was
looking for. Fish. Cats and fish. They go
together — like pancakes and blueberry
syrup.

I can be very graceful when I want to be. Gracefully, I slipped inside the door. It wasn't easy. Those cats kept trying to trip me.

Inside, it was dark. It was cold. It smelled like fish. There was a reason for that. All around, there were trays of fish. They were packed in ice. They were staring at me.

Usually, I don't like fish. I avoid trays of fish, if I can. But I was on to something big. I stuck with it.

I searched high and low. I don't usually look through fish. It's not my style. There was a bluefish. There was a flounder. There was a swordfish. I heard a noise. I hid behind the swordfish. A man came out. He was holding a fish. He dumped it on a pile of ice.

The element of surprise has been known to catch many a catnapper. This was my chance. I sprang forward. "*You* are the catnapper," I accused.

"Blimey, y'little bloke, y'haff scairt me to death!" the man said. Something wasn't right. Do catnappers talk like that? I wasn't sure.

"Get y'er blimey self out'er here. And take y'er bloomin' cats, too!" he shouted.

I thought it best to leave. I ran outside. I looked at the sign over the door. It said: **AL TEABERRY'S HOUSE OF REAL ENGLISH FISH AND CHIPS.** I think I just met Mr. Teaberry.

Oh, well. Like I said. I didn't ask to be a famous detective. I didn't ask to find Crumpet. But I didn't give up, either.

I kept walking toward Richard's
house. Orwell was coming down the
street. "Yech! You smell like a fish," he
said. Orwell has a way with words.
Sometimes I wish Orwell didn't have a
way with words.

"Did you take Richard's cat?" I asked him.

"Are you referring to a large black and white cat?" asked Orwell.

I nodded.

"Are you referring to a cat with long nails, who is fond of using them?" continued Orwell.

I nodded again.

"Are you referring to a cat who likes to hiss?" he asked.

"That's right. That sounds like Crumpet," I said.

"Then the answer is *no*—I did not take Crumpet. And you are crazy if you think for one minute that I would take that nasty creature," Orwell said.

I had to agree with Orwell. He had a point. But a good detective leaves no stone unturned. (I read that somewhere.)

I kept on walking. Walking helps me think. Walking and thinking go together — like pancakes and blueberry syrup. I thought about what Orwell said. He was right. Who would want Crumpet? Not me. Not Mr. Teaberry. Not Orwell.

Soon I came to the park. I sat down to think. Sitting is also good for thinking. I closed my eyes. Suddenly, I wasn't alone. I felt someone staring at me. Slowly, I opened my eyes. I saw two feet and four paws. The feet were wearing pink and purple plaid sneakers. There is only one person who has sneakers like that. Victoria. The paws were brown. They belonged to Victoria's dog, Honeybee.

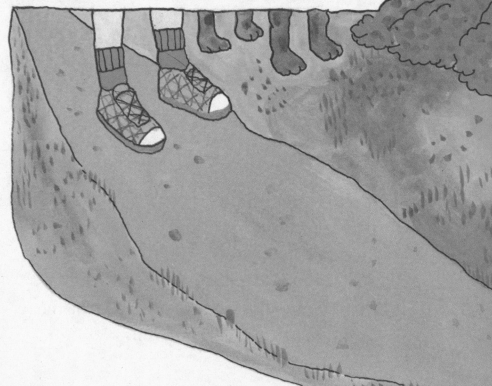

"What are you doing?" asked Victoria.

"Thinking," I said.

"You don't look like it. You look like you're sleeping," said Victoria.

"I am trying to figure out what happened to Crumpet, Richard's cat," I said.

"Oh."

"Hey, maybe you can help me," I said to her. "Let's make believe . . ."

"You mean 'pretend'?" asked Victoria.

"Yeah."

"I don't like to pretend," said Victoria.

"Okay, Victoria," I said, "let's just say it's a game, and we suppose you're a cat."

"I don't like games, and I'm not a cat," said Victoria.

"Victoria," I said, "go away."

"I can't stay anyhow," said Victoria. "I've got more important things to do. Honeybee is very hungry. We have to go and feed you, don't we, Honeybee?"

To tell you the truth, I wasn't too sorry to see Victoria go. A person like that can throw a real monkey wrench into a detective's detection. But there was one thing that Victoria said. It stuck in my mind. Maybe it was the clue I was looking for.

When I got to Richard's, he was
sitting on the front steps.

"Did you find out who took Crumpet?"
he asked.

"I found out who did *not* take Crumpet: not me, not Mr. Teaberry, not Victoria, and not Orwell," I said. "And if nobody took her, then she is hiding out! And if she is hiding out, she must be getting hungry!"

I was on to something big. I went into
the kitchen. I poured some milk into a
bowl. "These are her favorites," said
Richard, putting some tuna and liverwurst
into another bowl.

We put the bowls on the front steps.
We hid in the bushes. I don't usually hide
in bushes. There are more comfortable
places to hide. But this was a stake out.

We waited. Soon I saw something
black and white. With claws.

"It's Crumpet!" said Richard.

"Quiet! We'll follow her when she's
done eating," I said.

Wouldn't you know it? Crumpet is
a slow eater. And those bushes were
beginning to bother me. Finally, all the
food was gone. Crumpet looked around to
make sure no one was following her. She
went to the side of the house. She went to
the back of the house. She crept down the
cellar steps. She disappeared.

We tiptoed down the steps into the cellar. It was dark. We heard a hiss. A Crumpet-sounding hiss. I turned on the light. There, on an old blanket, was Crumpet. But she wasn't alone. There were six little Crumpets with her.

Well, I don't have to tell you Richard was happy. "Guess what?" he said. He didn't wait for me to guess. "I'm going to give you one of Crumpet's kittens. It will be your reward for solving the mystery of the missing cat. How would that be?"

To tell you the truth, I wasn't overjoyed. "I'll tell you what would be better," I said, "a nice plate of pancakes with blueberry syrup."

Well, that's how it happened. These things get around. It's a funny thing. The next thing you know, I'm famous. It's one case after another. It turns out this neighborhood's got a lot of mysteries waiting to be solved. And I'm the one to solve them! Mark my words.